STUART HILL

FIRE! FIRE!

A STRUGGLE FOR SURVIVAL IN
THE GREAT FIRE
OF LONDON, 1666

SCHOLASTIC

PROLOGUE

I don't know how long I ran through the burning streets of the city. The sky was dark with clouds of smoke, so I couldn't guess the time and any church bells that still rang the hours had either been burnt down or their chimes were lost in the deafening roar of the fire. I could see no landmarks to guide me and I soon lost my way. One burning street looks much the same as another.

As I ran, I coughed and spluttered in the smoke. My hands were black with soot and I guessed that my face would be in the same state. My clothes were scorched too and peppered with small black holes where sparks had hit me and burned through the cloth. Some of these sparks had reached my skin and I could feel tiny burns all over my back, shoulders, arms and legs.

I knew I couldn't go on for much longer; my chest ached from the smoke and fumes and I could hardly breathe. I had to get out of the fire and find a safe place to rest. Eventually I was forced to slow down by sheer exhaustion until I was barely shuffling forwards, pushed along by the crowds of people who were still cramming the streets as they ran from the fire. Despite feeling totally worn out, I forced myself to keep looking, to keep searching for any sign of him. Where was he? Why couldn't I find him? But really I knew it was impossible. I suppose I secretly knew it always had been. How could I have hoped to find one individual in this huge city? Especially when the city was engulfed in flames?

The fire was closing in on everyone and everything. It would kill all living things in its path. What chance did any of us have against the fury of the flames?

CHAPTER 1

My name's Tom Hubbard and I'm twelve years old...
I think. At least that's what my mother told me, but we
hardly ever discussed unimportant things like when
I was born. We were too busy trying to find enough
food to live on to worry about details like that. But
everything changed when I got a job in the household
kitchens of Master Samuel Pepys. My mother was so
happy knowing that I'd be warm, well-fed and safe.

I even have my own room; although I'm the youngest
of all the servants I can shut my door on everyone and
have some space to myself. Most of the maids and
serving men have to share with others in the attics or
cellars, or sleep in whatever space they can find next to
the kitchen fire.

"I can die in peace now," Mother said to me when
she heard about my new job. And sadly, within a
few months she did die, though not in peace. Like

thousands of others in the summer of last year, she died horribly of the plague. I was working in the kitchens at the time so even now I don't know where she's buried. I was told that her body was taken away in a cart with dozens of others and thrown into one of the plague pits where hundreds of people were buried together. So many people died and so quickly, there just wasn't time or even space to bury them individually. The only thing I could do was to go to the nearest plague pit that had been filled in and lay some flowers on the huge mound of earth that covered it. I hope that mother understood that I did my best to say goodbye to her properly.

....

My new master, Samuel Pepys (it's pronounced 'Peeps'), was one of the most important people in London. He worked as Secretary to the Navy. I didn't know what that meant exactly, but I knew it had something to do with the warships that kept our country safe from enemies and that my new master was very good at his job.

Of course that didn't make much difference to me. Working all day in the heat and steam of the kitchens

I never saw any of the important people who came to visit the house. I just had to help the cooks and kitchen maids get everything ready for the wonderful meals they ate. My day started early at five o'clock in the morning, and sometimes didn't finish until the clocks were striking ten o'clock at night! I knew I was lucky to have a job in such an important household, but the work was hard. Things were made easier by my friend, Pip. He was the kitchen dog, a small black and white terrier whose job it was to kill any rats and mice that tried to steal food from the pantries and storerooms. He shared a sleeping space with me near the fires when I first arrived in the house and didn't have my own room. Pip could always make me smile when I felt sad about my mother, and he'd growl a warning if anyone tried to steal our place next to the fire.

But then came a day when everything changed.

....

I was scrubbing the kitchen floor and the noise of the stiff brush bristles on the flagstones meant that I didn't hear Master Pepys come into the kitchen. He was talking to the head steward about a dinner he was planning for some important friends.

"Will you stop that infernal noise!" a voice suddenly shouted and a hand pulled me roughly to my feet.

When I realized it was Master Pepys I was terrified. I could easily lose my job if he got angry with me and then I could be thrown onto the streets with nowhere to live! I started to say sorry, but he waved me to silence while he straightened his wig which had slipped to one side when he'd grabbed me. All fashionable men wore these long wigs, including the king and his court. But as my master settled the hairpiece in place he suddenly stopped and stared at me.

"What's your name, boy?" he asked, his eyes narrowing.

"Tom Hubbard, sir," I almost whispered, dreading what he might say next.

"And are you fit and well? Can you run, boy? Can you stand up straight? Are you intelligent?"

"Yes, sir. To all of those things," I answered, my voice coming back strongly as I guessed that perhaps an opportunity could be coming my way.

"Hmmm…" was the only reply Master Pepys gave.

Then he turned back to the head steward. "A man of my standing needs a pageboy, Richards. Would this boy do?"

The head steward looked at me sternly. "He's bright and he'll clean up reasonably. With a bit of training I think he'd do well enough."

"Good," Master Pepys said. "Teach him his manners, get him a suit of clothes from the wardrobes and then send him to me. How long will it take?"

"A week should make him presentable as long as he only has to stand still when needed and run errands when asked. The rest he can learn as he goes along."

I stood listening with my mouth open in excited amazement and then, remembering I was supposed to look like a pageboy, I snapped it shut again.

I was both terrified and thrilled at the thought of being Master Pepys' personal servant, but I was now also determined to be the best pageboy there had ever been. It just goes to show how unexpected things can happen. When Master Pepys had grabbed me I thought I was about to lose my job, and now here I was in a new and much better position!

....

That all happened three months ago and now I have several fine suits of clothes and my own room in the attic, so I can be called whenever Master Pepys needs me. If only my mother had lived long enough to see all of this. She would've been so proud.

CHAPTER 2

Having my own room meant that I no longer shared a sleeping place by the fires with Pip, the kitchen dog. But now every night he leaves his post in the pantries and sneaks up to my room using the backstairs, and I let him sleep on my bed. He's a kind little creature who was my only friend when I first arrived in the house, and now he's like family. I've no one else in all the world but him. I always make sure he gets enough to eat and take him for walks around the city whenever I have time off. We love exploring the streets together.

....

Then one hot and dry September night a strange thing happened. Pip jumped up off the bed and started to scratch at my door. As I sat up to see what he wanted, I heard Jane, the head housemaid, clattering down the wooden stairs. She had the room next to mine and must have woken the dog as she rushed off. I wondered what she was doing making such a racket in the middle of the night.

I told Pip to be quiet and placed him back on the bed as I went to find out what was happening. I could hear Jane bustling down the flights of stairs ahead of me and I hurried after her. I caught up with her two floors down, just as she arrived at my master and mistress's bedroom.

"What's going on?" I asked in a hoarse whisper, but she ignored me and hammered on the door. I knew it had to be something really important if she was prepared to wake them up. What could it be?

The loud snores coming from the bedroom suddenly stopped as Jane knocked again and a sleepy and confused voice called out: "Who's there…? What's wrong…?"

Without waiting Jane pushed the door open and rushed in. I immediately followed, in case Master Pepys should need me… but also because I was desperate to know what was going on!

"I'm sorry, Sir and Madam," Jane gabbled. "But I

thought you should know... there's a huge fire burning across the city!" She pointed out of the window and down towards where London Bridge crossed the river.

Master Pepys leapt out of bed, his nightshirt billowing like a sail on a warship and hurried over to the window to look. I moved to stand behind him and peered round his wide frame to see what was going on.

Far off in the distance, over the crowded roofs of all the houses and the tall spires of the churches, I could see a red glow in the sky somewhere near the Billingsgate area of the city. My mistress joined us, making a small crowd of four around the narrow window.

"Is that all?!" Master Pepys demanded, as he saw the flames. "A dog could wee on that and put it out!"

"Perhaps Pip could help," I said with a quiet snigger, not really wanting to get Jane into trouble.

My mistress resettled her nightcap that had fallen over one eye. "Really, Jane, what a fuss about nothing! And so early... what time is it?"

"Three o'clock!" Master Pepys exploded. "Next time you see a fire, wait until it's knocking on our door with fiery hands before you disturb us!"

Jane looked embarrassed and miserable, but

managed a curtsey before apologizing and withdrawing. I followed her out and closed the door quietly behind me.

"Never mind," I said, trying to be comforting. "You did what you thought best."

She nodded but said nothing. I went back to my room and tried to settle Pip down again, but he jumped about excitedly until I picked him up. I stood on my bed so that I could peer out of the tiny window that was set into the sloping ceiling. I could still see the glow of the fire in the sky and thought that it might have got a little bigger and brighter, but it was hard to tell. Pip seemed interested and snuffled at the glass, so I lifted the handle and pushed the small window open. Immediately the warm night air rushed in, bringing with it the faint scent of smoke

"London's burning, Pip," I said and he whimpered in reply.

CHAPTER 3

I went back to bed and then woke again at my usual time and got up. It was five o'clock on September 2nd and the sun had not yet risen, but there was enough light in the sky for me to dress without needing to light a candle. Master Pepys wouldn't be up for another three hours or so, but in the mornings I would help lay the fires in the kitchen and fetch and carry for the cooks and kitchen maids. Before I went down the service stairs, I stood on my bed with Pip in my arms again and gazed out of the window to where I'd seen the glow of the fire the night before. Only now it wasn't a glow. It had definitely grown and spread in the last few hours and a huge plume of smoke rose up from it like a storm cloud. A shiver of fear went through me.

I'd seen lots of fires in the streets before, but they were usually put out quickly. This one had been burning all night and was still getting bigger. I felt a strange knotting in my stomach as I thought of all the people who could have been trapped by the flames and burned to death. And the knot got tighter when I realized that if it spread even further the fire could even reach Master Pepys' house.

"My God, I hope they put it out soon, Pip. Otherwise we might be looking for a new home…" I paused and shivered in fear before adding: "if we're still alive that is!"

Pip gave a small yap as though he understood what I'd said. But then he started to dance around. He needed to empty his bladder as usual so I quickly opened the door and followed the sound of his skittering claws down the back service stairs. When I reached the ground floor I slipped out into the garden to make sure Pip came back in and didn't run off now that the fire was getting bigger. I couldn't bear the thought of him getting lost in the chaos of fire and smoke. I don't know what I'd do without him. As I leaned against the house and took a deep breath of the morning air I was immediately hit by the smell of burning. Master Pepys' house stands on Seething Lane; it's on a hill and looks down on most of the city north of the river, so I was able to look out over the houses south towards the

Thames and Billingsgate where the fire was.

The billows of black smoke still rose up and the dawn sky was made much brighter by the flames I could now see raging over the roofs of the houses.

A wind moved through the old apple trees in the garden, sweeping from the south. It brought with it the distant sounds of roaring, crackling flames and what sounded like hundreds of people shouting and even screaming. Pip appeared at my feet at last, but instead of running madly in circles with his usual wide-mouthed panting, he snuggled up to my legs and sniffed worriedly at the smoky air.

"Come on, boy," I said, opening the door back into the kitchens. "The fire's a long way off and it'll be out before the sun rises."

The dog hurried inside and I followed him, glancing over my shoulder at the distant flames, not sure whether I believed my own words or not.

....

The conversation amongst the kitchen maids and boys was all about the fire as we started the ovens and prepared for the day ahead. But soon deliveries began to arrive from different shops and suppliers throughout the city, and with each delivery came news about the fire. Soon we found out that the flames were spreading quickly and that overnight over three hundred houses had been destroyed. It had started in a bakery in Pudding Lane and had now spread to Fish Lane and was heading for London Bridge. Nobody knew how many people had died, or if any had at all. There were so many different stories it was impossible to know what to think. But remembering the shouts and screams that'd been carried by the wind into the garden earlier, I couldn't believe that nobody had been hurt.

....

When the time came to get my master up for the day, I almost ran up the stairs, bursting with the news.

"Three hundred houses destroyed!" he bellowed, as I helped him on with his shirt. "Has no one put the blessed thing out yet?!"

He hopped to the window with one shoe on while I followed after with the other. "Saints and sausages!

It's spread!" he gasped as he saw the huge billows of smoke rolling up into the sky. "The king must be told! My coat; my wig; we must be off!"

"Not without your trousers, sir," I said quietly.

"What? Oh, no… not without my trousers," he agreed, staring down at his bare legs. "The white silk ones, Tom. And the blue sash."

I was so excited that I was going to see the king that I almost tripped over the trousers as I fetched them from the clothes chest. London was burning and that should have been the only thing in my thoughts, but I couldn't help it. It wasn't every day that a boy from a poor background like me got to go to a royal palace and stand before a king!

When we were finally ready, we burst out of the house and I took up the proper place of a pageboy, two paces behind Master Pepys. But as we went down the hill the streets began to fill with people and every sort of handcart and horse-drawn wagon you could think of as folk ran from the fire, taking with them as many of their belongings as they could. It was so crowded I drew level with my master and held onto his coat, not wanting us to get separated as we fought our way through the running crowds.

The bitter scent of smoke was much stronger now and the sounds of screaming and crackling flames wafted over us with every breath of wind. I looked south towards the fire and wondered how far away it was. Maybe not more than a couple of miles.

"Quick, Tom, to the Tower of London, that's the best place to see this fire clearly and in safety," my master said, and we both hurried as fast as we could down towards Tower Hill and the ancient fortress that stood on the banks of the Thames.

When we arrived beneath the stone-built walls we found the streets still packed with people all hurrying about in a state of panic. We forced our way through the crowds until we got to the gates that were guarded by soldiers. Master Pepys knew the Commander of the Tower so we were soon allowed in and then up onto the walls where we looked eastwards and saw the fire raging through the city. I gasped in horror at the terrible sight and for a moment Master Pepys bowed his head as we both thought of the poor people fleeing from the flames.

We could clearly see London Bridge too and already the flames had burst through the great gateway that defended the road leading onto the bridge itself. We could see people, tiny as ants from this distance, running back towards the safety of the south bank where the fire hadn't reached. But others were bravely standing against it. They seemed to have formed a line and were handing buckets of water forward to throw onto the flames that had taken hold of the wooden bridge. But we could see it was hopeless. Soon there was a great creaking and groaning and as we watched a whole section of the bridge fell into the Thames with a mighty roar. Many of those fighting the fire must have fallen with it, but though I stared long and hard at the churning waters, I saw nobody swimming away.

I think I screamed aloud in horror, but my voice was lost amongst all the other cries. People were dying in this fire and nobody seemed able to stop it!

Master Pepys fell grimly silent for a moment, but then took a deep breath. "Come, Tom. We must away to the king and tell His Majesty of all we have seen."

I thought that the king must surely have been told all about it already, but I said nothing and just nodded. Then I followed as my master hurried down the steps, heading towards the river and the palace.

....

When we arrived at the quayside where we hoped to get a boat to take us to Whitehall Palace, the crowds were even worse. People were shoving and crying and calling out to the boatmen who made a living ferrying passengers up and down the river. The crush was so great some people were pushed into the water and some of them couldn't swim, so their cries for help and splashing added to the terrible noise. Luckily the boatmen soon picked them up and hauled them to safety.

I shouted myself hoarse trying to get a boat, but my voice was lost amongst all the others. I waved and jumped up and down as though I'd gone mad, but as everyone else was doing exactly the same this didn't make much difference either.

Eventually Master Pepys himself stepped forward, looking splendid in his fine clothes and huge wig and his stomach curving outwards like the prow of a warship. He struck his long walking cane sharply on the stonework of the quayside and drew breath, filling his lungs so that he swelled up like a sail bursting with the power of hurricane.

"BOATMAN! BOATMAN! TO ME! TO ME! I HAVE A JOURNEY TO MAKE TO THE KING HIMSELF!"

His voice rose up and over everything like a fanfare from a dozen trumpets and no fewer than three boats immediately headed towards us. We both hurried down the steps and jumped into the nearest one before anyone else could take our place. Soon we were powering out into the flow of the river.

Within a few strokes of the oar we were well out on the water, and looking along the riverbank we could see the fire without any buildings hiding it from view. All the streets around the road leading to London Bridge were ablaze and the wind was blowing strongly, driving the fire into more houses. It rose high up into the sky like a great forest of flames, with trunks and branches and twigs and leaves of fire. Rising up over it all was a massive, billowing cloud of black smoke that was spreading itself wide over the city – from Tower Street and then eastwards towards the distant spire of Saint Paul's Cathedral – turning the daytime to night for those beneath it.

The stench of the burning mixed and mingled with the screams and cries of the people running from the flames, as though flocks of terrified birds sang in a fire forest. "To the Palace of Whitehall!" Master Pepys said to the boatman and the man immediately hauled on his oars, driving us quickly through the water.

CHAPTER 4

We arrived at the watergate – the entranceway that led from the river directly into the huge building of Whitehall Palace itself. This was the first time I'd come to see King Charles II, and I'm proud to say that my master was well known at the palace so no one stopped him or asked him his business as we hurried through the winding corridors up towards the place where the king held court.

For a moment I stopped and just stared at all the incredible beauty around me. But Master Pepys soon hurried me on. The contrast between the dirt and grime of the streets and the colours and richness of the palace was amazing. The bright shining gilding that covered even the wooden parts of the tables and chairs in gold reminded me for a moment of the flames that were raging through the streets of the city along the river. But I was soon distracted by the beautiful pictures that covered the walls of the corridors we hurried along. It was all so amazing. I thought Master Pepys's home was beautiful, but the palace was something else entirely. It was like the difference between a well-made and decorated pottery cup, and a wine glass made of the finest, clearest crystal. Some of the paintings showed scenes of faraway mountains and cities as though they were windows opening onto different worlds, and others were portraits of people who seemed to stare at us as we passed by.

Everything was so quiet too after the chaos of the fire; the roaring of the flames and screaming of the people were blocked by the thick stonework of the palace walls. In fact the only sound I could hear was the noise our hurrying feet made over the polished wooden floors. But then at last we came to a pair of huge doors where two guards stood, holding their spears across the entranceway.

My master stepped forward importantly and spoke with confidence. "Samuel Pepys Esquire, Secretary to the Navy and now bearer of bad news about the progress of a fire that is destroying parts of our city. All seen and witnessed by my good self and ready to be told to the king … oh, and this is Tom Hubbard, my pageboy and servant."

I stood as straight as I could and felt in that moment almost as important as my master. The guards stamped to attention, withdrew their spears and, as if by magic, the doors opened behind them.

Before us was a huge room full of men and women dressed in colours as bright as flowers in a garden. Everyone was chattering and laughing brightly and when they finished their conversations they bowed or curtsied deeply before moving on to someone else to talk with. I couldn't help thinking of the burning streets along the river where people were dying in the flames or running in fear of their lives.

At the top of the room in the distance I could see a canopy of velvet that hung over a gilded chair where a tall man sat.

Master Pepys surged forward across the room, ignoring the questions that were flung at us, until we stood before the gilded chair. Here he bowed deeply, waving his hand before him as though cleaning dust from his shoes. I bowed too, though without the dusting, then I stood up again and found I could hardly breathe. I was standing before the king himself … the king! The most important man in all the land! His wig was so long the ends of it almost rested in his lap where two small spaniels sat, and his clothes glowed with gold and brilliant colours. For a moment I thought I was going to faint, but then I pulled myself together. What a fool I'd look if I collapsed in a heap in front of the king.

"Pepys," His Majesty said quietly. "What news?"

"Of a great fire, my Lord. It spreads without stopping. London Bridge has collapsed into the Thames. When I awoke this morning over three hundred houses had been destroyed and by now many more must have been swallowed up by its fury."

"Yes, I've been told something of a fire, but no details. Obviously it has got out of hand." I looked at His Majesty, amazed that he seemed so calm and unworried. But then I realized that perhaps he really wasn't worried. After all, the fire would have to get much worse before it threatened the king in his palace with its high stone walls. But I did think he should have been worried for the people he ruled, people who were running from the flames even as we stood before his throne.

The king turned then and murmured to a richly

dressed man who stood next to the gilded chair. The man was so like him he could only be the king's brother. King Charles turned back to us.

"The Duke of York agrees with me, something must be done. Pepys, go to Thomas Bloodworth, the mayor, and tell him he must pull down houses to make a firebreak. He's rumoured to be somewhere near Saint Paul's Cathedral. Take a carriage from the royal stables and fly like the wind."

He was then distracted by one of the small spaniels that had got itself entangled in his long wig. When he looked up again, he seemed surprised to see us. "Still here, Pepys? Go… like the wind."

My master bowed again but then asked: "shall I tell him that help is on the way, Your Majesty… perhaps in the form of men to fight the fire?"

The king seemed surprised to be asked a question. "There may be help, presently. I'm considering sending in the army under the command of the Duke of York, though I've not yet decided which regiments to appoint to the role, or how many."

His Majesty then picked up an embroidered glove that lay in his lap and flicked it at us as though we were flies bothering him.

Master Pepys bowed again and then we were hurrying back through the room and out into the maze of corridors that flew by in a blur of colour, gilded furniture and beautiful pictures. Then we were out into a wide yard where carriages stood with horses already harnessed and waiting.

I guessed most of them must have belonged to the ladies and gentlemen who'd been in the room with the king, but we didn't pause to think about what they'd say if we took their carriage into the fire. We just leapt into the nearest one while my master roared at the coachman to go "On the orders of the king!" Suddenly we jolted and bumped to a start and then surged forward, gathering speed. My heart was racing!

Soon we were clattering through the streets and heading straight for the fire.

....

The coachman seemed to enjoy carrying out the king's orders. As we got closer to the flames he galloped through the crowds of Londoners running from the destruction, lashing out with his whip to clear a way and shouting that he was on a mission for "His Majesty himself!"

People dived out of the way of the flashing hooves of the two horses as we surged on through the smoke and flying sparks, getting ever closer to St Paul's, which rose up in the distance like a huge stone ship.

My heart was pounding as though I was the one running instead of the horses. I swayed and rocked inside the coach, while Master Pepys hung on to his wig, which flapped like a bird in the wind.

I was excited and terrified at the same time; the closer we got to the inferno the more likely we were to die. But we were going to help – maybe even stop the fire!

"What did the king mean when he said the mayor should knock down houses to make a firebreak? What exactly is a firebreak?" I asked.

Master Pepys glanced at me through his wig that was still flapping in the wind. "A firebreak is a wide gap made in the line of houses. It would stop the fire spreading further because there wouldn't be anything left to burn."

"Oh, I see… that's a good idea." I said.

"Well yes, it is, as long as whoever knocks down the houses also takes away all of the wood and other material that the building was made of, that can still burn."

"Ah, yes," I replied. "And that would be hard work and very difficult."

"Exactly so, Tom," Master Pepys said, and looked at me meaningfully.

....

We were now galloping along Fleet Street back towards Tower Hill and I could see the fire dancing over the roofs of the houses, towering up into the air in a wall of blazing light. It almost sounded like a storm at sea: roaring, hissing and crashing. As it burned, it seemed to draw the air into it, creating a huge wind, as though the flames needed to breathe. But the wind only drove the fire along, leaping from roof to roof like a living creature and sending up huge billows of smoke and deadly sparks.

Now the horses started to throw their heads about and look very scared as they saw the burning buildings more clearly and the stench of smoke got stronger. Soon we came to a complete standstill as the horses reared up and screamed.

"It's no good, sir, they'll go no nearer," the coachman said regretfully, and we were forced to climb down. We were plunged into the crowds of people hurrying by with bags and boxes stuffed with what they could save from the flames. Master Pepys pressed a coin into the coachman's hand to show his thanks, and then, holding onto his wig, he began to battle against the flow of people as though against the strongest tide. I followed behind, hanging onto my master's coattails.

"Not far now, Tom," he bellowed over the noise. "The king said Master Bloodworth was somewhere near Saint Paul's."

"But how will we find him, sir, in all this… this… mix and muddle and clatter?" I shouted back as I coughed and spluttered in the smoke.

Master Pepys carried on pressing forwards, like a man wading through a river. "I'm not sure… but we must try. It is our duty to the king."

I found myself thinking that if the king wanted to give orders to Master Bloodworth, the mayor of his city, then perhaps he should find him himself. But then I pushed such thoughts out of my head, horrified by my treacherous thoughts.

Suddenly there was a huge blast, as though a barrel of gunpowder had exploded somewhere in the flames. Several people in the crowds threw themselves to the ground. I too ducked down, terrified, but my master carried on moving forward as though nothing had happened and I had to follow.

I could feel the heat now almost like a solid wall. We both paused for a moment as we got used to the hot air forcing its way up our nostrils and then down into our lungs.

"Saints and sausages, Tom," Master Pepys gasped. "I feel my words should burst into fire as I speak!"

I nodded and looked around at the blazing buildings. We were on Fleet Street, a main highway that was mercifully wider than many of the roads in this old part of the city. But as we struggled on through the pressing crowds and the heat and smoke, we somehow got pushed away from the wide road of the main route and into the tangled and twisted side streets that led south towards the River Thames. I don't know how far out of our way we went because the streets were like a maze. We also had to keep alert as buildings collapsed into the street around us and filled all the open space with rubble. We both took out handkerchiefs and held them over our mouths as we scurried on like ants in a grassfire. But then suddenly a loud CRACK!!! echoed through the air and we skidded to a stop. A wall as high as a cliff slowly toppled forward and fell with a mighty crash into the street.

The cloud of smoke and dust billowed over us, like a strangely hot winter fog. We both coughed and spluttered, but Master Pepys soon began to move forward once more and I hung onto his coattails again, scared of getting lost in the firestorm.

Soon we came to an area where the fire had already burned away most of the houses and, though it was still mightily hot and smoke billowed around us in dense clouds, we could hurry on much more quickly.

Then ahead I could see where the fire must have been blown around almost in a circle by the strong wind. Before we knew it we were walking through what looked like a tunnel of fire as houses on both sides of the street erupted into flames.

Worse even than the smoke and the heat were the cries and screams of people and what must have been animals. Many of those who lived in the buildings had obviously escaped, because now these roads were empty of everything apart from the terrible choking fumes. I didn't like to think what could be happening to those who were screaming. They must've been trapped in some way, but there was nothing we could do – we couldn't have got through the heat and flames to rescue anyone. Besides, we were carrying the orders of the king himself and nothing could be allowed to delay those.

The wind was now blowing more and more strongly and the flames roared up as though a giant blacksmith was using massive bellows to stoke up his forge, ready to melt the world away to nothing. I clung on to Master Pepys' coat even more tightly as I tried not to panic, and noticed he was holding his wig over his face as well as his handkerchief to keep the smoke out of his lungs. Unfortunately I was too young for a wig, and they were also too expensive for a pageboy. But just as I was staring in envy at my master, he glanced back at me and, realizing I was coughing and spluttering more than him, immediately handed me the wig.

"Here, Tom, use this. It's my second best wig so don't get it too snotty!" He shouted over the roaring fire.

I took it from him gratefully and held its thick curls over my mouth and nose. Then, finally, the way ahead cleared and we found ourselves on a part of the street where the flames hadn't reached. The smoke rolled away and Saint Paul's Cathedral loomed up before us, rising high into the sky like a mountain.

We headed as straight for it as we could and at last emerged back onto the wider way of Fleet Street. The road led directly to the cathedral and, within a few minutes, we arrived safely. The area around the huge church was still untouched by the fire and we hurried forwards into a space that was free of smoke and flames. For a moment we paused to breathe in air that wasn't quite as smoky and to enjoy the peace of an area that wasn't yet in flames. Many houses to the north and west still stood untouched, but the fire was heading towards them rapidly.

"Those are the buildings that must be demolished if the conflagration is to be stopped!" said Master Pepys, waving his hand at them.

I guessed that 'conflagration' was another word

for an enormous fire, and I looked out at the area of housing that had to be pulled down by order of the king.

Then, almost as though we'd made it happen just by talking about it, shouting voices rose up and suddenly with a CRACK and a CRASH one of the houses fell to the ground, disappearing in a billow of dust and disturbing the strange calm that had settled over the place.

We stood staring, our mouths hanging open. Then we saw a gang of men appear from the billowing cloud carrying long iron poles, hammers and huge spades. All of them were covered in dust, but one was wearing something that might once have been a fine coat. On his head was a wig so dirty it looked like a spaniel's ears after it's been rolling in mud.

"Look, Tom, I do believe... yes, I think I'm right... I'm almost certain that's Master Bloodworth, the mayor!"

The strange dirty figure saw us, strolled over and gave a deep bow. "Do I have the pleasure of the company of Master Samuel Pepys, Secretary to His Majesty's Navy?"

"Indeed you do, sir," my master answered, returning

the bow. "And do I have the pleasure of the company of Master Thomas Bloodworth, the Lord Mayor of London?"

"I am the very same," the Mayor answered. "May I ask the nature of your business?"

"Certainly you may. I have come on a mission from His Majesty the King to convey his direct order that you should demolish houses in the path of the conflagration in order to create a firebreak and so quench its power."

I listened to the fine language between the two gentlemen and felt myself tiny and unimportant before such good manners and wealth. But then I looked south towards the river where the fire raged and people screamed in fear and agony. I also looked at the filth and grime on the mayor's clothes and I realized that the fire cared nothing for good manners, fine speeches and money. If you were caught in its flames you would die in terror and pain, whether you were the richest person in England... or the poorest. For some reason that made me feel a little better. We're all the same, it's just that some are lucky enough to have wealth and power. But not even that could save you from terrible accidental happenings like fires.

The mayor now smiled at my master, his teeth brilliantly white against the grime all over his face. "Your mission has been without purpose, sir, for as you have just witnessed, I have been demolishing houses for the last few hours."

"Indeed yes," said Master Pepys. "His Majesty will be most pleased."

"Then when you inform him of my hard work, you may also tell him that I am returning home to sleep, as I have been up all the night destroying people's homes."

And with that, Mayor Bloodworth bowed deeply again, almost fell, and then turned and walked slowly away.

My master watched him leave in silence and then drew a deep breath and sighed. "Do you know, Tom, we serve kings out of a sense of loyalty and with a deep pride, but there are times when I believe that we servants could claim we deserve better masters."

I'm not exactly sure what my master meant by this, but I think he was saying that perhaps His Majesty could sometimes be a better king.

He then stepped closer to me and took his wig from where it lay around my shoulders, now that I didn't need it to protect my lungs from smoke.

"But," Master Pepys went on, as he placed the slightly crumpled and grubby wig on his head, "if ever you repeat to anyone the ridiculous idea that I am anything less than deeply loyal to the king and his family I will deny it, disown you and throw you out of my service."

"No such words would ever pass my lips, master," I replied quietly.

"Good, then let us walk briskly home. It's not too far from here to Seething Lane, and I've an appointment to keep for lunch"

CHAPTER 5

When we reached home, Master Pepys ordered a bath to be placed in his room and he soaked himself in warm water and soap for over an hour "to remove the foul stench of smoke from my flesh."

He told me that I must wash too as his luncheon guests wouldn't want to be attended by a pageboy who stank like a bonfire. There was no time or place for me to have a bath so I had to make do standing under the pump in the stable yard. While one of the grooms worked the handle, I scrubbed at myself with a brush usually used for cleaning the stable floor.

The weather was still fine and warm, as it had been all summer, but the water was freezing. I hurriedly dried and dressed myself while Pip sat close by, staring at me as though I was mad. The little dog had found me as soon as we returned home. He ran out of the kitchens wagging his tail and jumping about, but stopped playing suddenly when the roar of the fire came to us on the wind and the smell of burning got even stronger. He cowered down to the ground and whimpered, so I picked him up and cuddled him while he licked my face.

"It's all right, Pip, the fire won't reach here," I said, hoping desperately that I was right. "Master Pepys has heard that the king's brother is in charge of fighting it now and he has the army to help him."

I didn't know how soldiers were supposed to fight the raging fire with their muskets and swords, but obviously the king thought they'd do some good, and who was I to disagree.

I carried Pip back to the kitchens and he scampered off happily to hunt for rats in the cellars. But that was before the explosions began.

....

At luncheon I stood behind Master Pepys' chair and refilled his wine glass every time he emptied it… which was quite often. His guests were two very fine ladies and two equally impressive gentlemen, whose wigs hung in great long curls, falling from their heads like waterfalls.

From the dining room window I could clearly see the fire, though luckily it was still a good way off. But the thick smoke had spread wide over the city and had settled like a cloud over our house in Seething Lane.

"Oh yes, with no thought of any danger to my person, I accepted the king's orders and set off through the blazing streets to find Mayor Bloodworth," my master said loudly, as he told the tale of our earlier adventure through the fire to Saint Paul's.

"But weren't you afraid?" asked one of the ladies, peering at him through a pair of spectacles she had on a stick.

"Me, afraid?! Why, of course not. Though none of the gentlemen in the king's court would come with me. I had to brave the fires alone and unattended."

At this I jumped as though someone had poked me in the ribs. I hadn't meant to draw attention to myself but Master Pepys glanced at me over the back of his chair. "Ah yes, alone that is apart from Tom, here. He may be small, but he has the heart of a lion," he added and winked at me.

The lady looked at me through her glasses-on-a-stick. "This boy, Master Pepys? Brave? I'd find it easier to believe that a mouse would have the courage to fight an elephant and win," she said. While her friends sniggered into their wine glasses I decided that I didn't like her.

At that point a huge explosion sounded and everyone rushed over to the window. "What on earth could that have been?" asked the younger lady nervously.

"Oh, the mayor and the Duke of York are using gunpowder to blow up houses to make firebreaks. There's also the possibility that some old soldier still had weapons and gunpowder in his house and the fire's flaming fingers have found them," said my master. "But let us get back to our food before it cools upon our plates."

I went on staring out of the window, shuddering to think of the poor souls caught up in the fire, maybe dying at that very moment, while these beautifully dressed and refined people took luncheon as though nothing was happening. I could hear them chatting politely about nothing important and even laughing as I watched the flames destroying the lives and homes of the ordinary people of London.

"Tom, my glass," my master called and I was forced to hurry back to the table and pour wine.

The explosions continued to rattle the windows during the rest of the meal, and at one point I heard Pip's terrified barks echoing up from the kitchens. It was a real struggle not to excuse myself and run down to comfort him, but I was kept busy serving dainty sweets to everyone after they'd finished eating the savoury dishes.

As the meal and the fashionable chatter continued on, more and more explosions echoed over the city. Master Pepys began to show signs of worry. He stood at the window, glass in hand, watching the distant flames and muttering to himself. Then, after he failed to answer several questions they asked him, the guests finally decided they should leave. Their host seemed to be more interested in the fire than he was in them.

The fuss they made as they gathered their purses, walking canes and parasols reminded my master of his manners and he escorted them to the door. There the gentlemen bowed to each other and the ladies curtsied and everyone tried to find exactly the right way of saying goodbye to prove how refined they were.

When the door finally closed behind them, Master Pepys sighed in relief. "Sometimes it's hard work being a gentlemen, Tom," he said, before hurrying back to the window. I found myself thinking that it was probably far harder to be an ordinary working man or woman when your home was in flames and you were running for your life. But I said nothing. At heart Master Pepys was a good man and at least he was now beginning to show how worried he was about the fire as he stared out over the burning city.

For the rest of the afternoon my master watched the flames as they advanced through the city's streets. Something had changed in him. It was almost as though the explosions had somehow brought the reality of this fire home to him. Suddenly the fire was no longer something that was happening to other people in a different part of the city, now it was a disaster that threatened him and everything he owned.

At one point he even went out without me, telling me to "keep safe at home".

While my master was out of the house I spent as much of the afternoon as I could with Pip, sitting with him on my lap in the pantries. I made sure that I was hidden away at the back behind the table where the expensive Italian cheeses were stored under protecting cloth drapes. No one would find me there and think of work for me to do. The little dog was shivering with fright every time an explosion boomed over the sky, snuggling into my arms as closely as he could.

But I couldn't stay with him all day. All too soon the cry went up that my master finally returned home and wanted to know where I'd got to. I settled Pip in an old unused bread basket and left him with the cheeses. Reluctantly I went off to find out what I was needed for.

Master Pepys was in his study scribbling furiously at some papers.

"Ah, Tom, where have you been? No matter… " he said distractedly. "I met the king on the river on his royal barge and he told me the fire has spread further. The flames are even threatening Cheapside!" When I didn't react, he looked up from his scribbling with a look of horror on his face. "Did you hear me? Cheapside itself is in danger… the most fashionable area of the city where the richest and most important people live! Has this fire no respect?"

I made the right sort of noises but thought to myself that now the rich people were threatened, perhaps a real effort would be made to stop the flames.

"I've ordered wagons to come and take our furnishings and goods to safety." Master Pepys went on, interrupting my thoughts. "We can no longer just sit idly by and hope the flames will go away. Everything must be packed up and made ready so that we may leave as soon as needs be!"

....

For the rest of that evening and far into the night I helped the other servants pack all the household goods into crates. Everything from the lowliest vegetable knife to the finest painting was wrapped up and sealed into the huge wooden boxes. Soon the house echoed with emptiness.

By the time the moon had risen over the burning city, the main hallway was filled to the ceiling with crates. I was exhausted and almost fell asleep standing up! Master Pepys noticed this and kindly sent me off to bed, even though he and many of the older servants continued to work on into the night.

When I reached my room I found Pip cowering against the door. He was still shivering with fright and, just as I bent down to stroke him, another explosion echoed over the night sky. The Duke of York and his soldiers were obviously working hard to save Cheapside. But I was soon distracted as I had to grab Pip's collar before he ran off down the stairs in fright.

I picked him up and went into my room, closing the door securely behind me. I made a comfortable bed for him next to my pillow before reaching up to the small window in the sloping angle of the roof, opening it and looking out.

The fire was much nearer now, raging and writhing high up into the sky, like snakes of flame and light. The stench of smoke was almost more than I could bear, so I quickly closed the window and lay down on the bed fully dressed.

I must have fallen asleep immediately, because the next thing I knew I was being woken up by the uproar of the huge wagons arriving to take the household goods to safety. My bed must've been one of the few things that hadn't been packed away.

I immediately leapt up and hurried downstairs to help. I found the hall in a state of chaos. Some of the stronger servants carried the big crates out to the waiting wagons, and the rest hurried backwards and forwards with baskets full to the brim with cutlery, plates and anything else that could be fitted in.

Master Pepys must have found time to go to bed himself, because he was directing operations dressed only in his nightshirt, slippers and wig. Mrs Pepys stood at the front door waving the servants through to the waiting wagons and then back again. She too was in her nightgown and her large and complicated hairdo was securely anchored down with a white silk headscarf.

"Ah, Tom!" Master Pepys cried when he saw me. "Quick, down to the kitchens and bring up the basket of cheeses."

I did as I was told, and as I lugged the heavy basket back to the hall, I found my master waiting for me with a shovel in his hand.

"Splendid! Splendid! This way," he said, and I hurried after him as he led me through the main door and then round the side of the house to the small orchard we had. I had no idea what was going on.

"This will do, Tom. You can dig here."

"Dig, sir?"

"Yes. These Parmesan cheeses are far too delicate and

expensive to carry through the streets. They'll do very well buried here wrapped in linen and kept safe in these baskets."

I didn't think they'd 'do very well' if it rained, but as the weather was still warm and fine, perhaps they'd be safe. Though I couldn't even guess why my master was wasting time worrying about cheeses when so much was being destroyed by the fire.

As I dug down into the hard, dry soil, my master disappeared, but he soon returned with several bottles of wine.

"These can join the cheeses too, my lad. They're the finest sherry-wine, and easily disturbed by too much heat or fire."

By the time I'd dug a hole big enough, packed it with cheese and wine, and then filled the hole back up again, I was very hot and sweaty and coughing heavily as I breathed in the smoke and fumes. But there was no time to rest; Master Pepys led the way back into the house where I was soon busy fetching more baskets of goods from the kitchen and carrying them out to the four huge wagons that stood waiting on Seething Lane.

With all of the hard work and the rush and hurry I'd completely forgotten about Pip, until I heard a yap and there he was at my feet. He was shivering with fright, staring at the flames that were drawing ever nearer. "What are you doing here, Master Rat-catcher?" I asked the little dog. "I'll have to find a basket for you as soon as I get a moment and then get you stowed safely on one of the wagons."

It was just at that point that two of the kitchen porters staggered through the gates and out onto Seething Lane. They were carrying a huge wooden crate between them and it was obviously really heavy, judging by the amount of swearing that was going on. Then, as I watched, one of them lost his grip on the crate and it fell with an almighty crash, just as another explosion echoed over the sky.

Pip yelped in fright and, before I could do anything, he turned and ran off down the lane towards the fire.

"Pip, wait!" I shouted as he disappeared into the shadows. "PIP, COME BACK!" But it was no good, his small black and white form had been swallowed up by the dark and the smoke.

"Here you, give us a hand to clear up this mess," one of the porters called roughly, as he scrabbled about on his hands and knees trying to gather up all of the spilt crockery and pots.

But I shook my head. "I can't... I've got to find Pip!"

And before anyone could try and stop me, I ran after him, the best friend I had in the world.

CHAPTER 6

I heard the porters calling after me, but I ignored them. I couldn't let Pip get lost in a burning city! He must be so scared. But even though I ran as fast as I could, I couldn't even begin to guess where the dog had gone.

I ran on and on, down towards the river where the billowing clouds of smoke got slowly thicker and thicker. Amazingly, even though the fire had been burning for days, the roads were still full of people. Obviously many of them had stayed in their houses hoping that the fire would be put out, or the wind would blow it in a different direction before it reached their homes. But now the flames were eating up everything around them like a starving animal. So now, finally, they were filling the roads with handcarts, trying to save their goods and belongings.

For the past few days my every hour had been filled by the roar of fire, the stink of smoke and the screams of people, but now as I made my way down towards Lombard Street and the river, the noise and the smell got louder and stronger still.

Suddenly out of the corner of my eye I thought I saw a small black and white dog dodging down a side alley, and I ran after it as fast as I could. But it was no good – I lost sight of it almost as soon as I reached the alleyway. Everything was confusing and chaotic. The billowing smoke made it impossible to see more than a few feet ahead and the heat was almost unbearable. It was terrifying – at any moment a burning building could collapse on me or I could be swallowed up by flames as they blasted into the roadway, driven by the strong winds. I ran as fast as I could, as though I could escape all the dangers, but the faster I ran, the harder I breathed the smoke and fumes into my lungs, making me cough and splutter and stumble.

It got so bad I had to stop. I sank down on the doorstep of a house that wasn't yet burning, and tried to breathe slowly. A huge gust of hot wind howled along the street, clearing the smoke for a moment and making it easier to breathe. I leaned back against the door, catching my breath and it was then that I heard the calling voice. I don't know why or how I heard it over all of the other screams and shouts, but I did. Whoever it was, they sounded old and tired and without hope.

"Will no one help me?" the voice called again, but it was quieter now, as though they had almost given up.

I was almost angry to be distracted from my search for Pip, but I couldn't leave somebody to burn to death.

"Where are you?" I called, climbing to my feet. No one answered.

"I'll try and help, but I have to know where you are!" I looked around for someone else who might help, but there was no one about.

"In here!" the voice came again, sounding surprised and relieved. "I'm in here. Behind the black door."

I looked across the street to where a black door was half hidden by a fallen beam of wood. I was scared of course – who wouldn't be in the middle of a burning city? But there was no time to think about it really. Someone needed help and I had to give it. The house wasn't on fire yet, but all the buildings around it were ablaze. I ran over to the fallen joist and grabbed an end, but it was too heavy for me.

Unlike a few minutes earlier, there were now lots of

people hurrying by, fleeing from the flames. But when I called to them for help they just ignored me and carried on their way.

"Your door's blocked. Can you climb out of the window?" I finally called

"I don't know… perhaps, if you help me."

It's amazing how quickly people can get used to horrible situations. If you'd told me a few days earlier that I'd be standing in a street where fires burned fiercely and that, instead of running away, I'd be trying to help somebody escape from their house, I'd have thought you were mad. And yet, here I was, my skin scorched by the heat of the flames, trying to think how I could get into a house that was about to catch fire!

Then I thought of my mother. I couldn't protect her from the plague, but perhaps if I could help this person that would in some way make up for not saving the woman who'd brought me into the world and loved me and looked after me for the first twelve years of my life.

I could only hope. My mother was gone, and wherever she was I had no way of knowing if she knew what I was doing. In the end, all I could do was shrug to myself and get on with it. I couldn't let somebody die in a fire if I could do something about it. With that thought, I ran to the window, smashed it open with a fallen roof tile and quickly climbed in.

Inside it was dark and so full of smoke I couldn't see a thing. "Where are you, can you make your way towards me?"

For a moment nothing happened, but then I saw a shadow moving towards me. I hurried forward and grabbed the hand that I could now was grasping blindly at the air.

"This way," I said. "Let's get out before we're baked alive!"

"You'll have to help me, I don't think I can climb very easily."

The voice was quiet and cracked. Peering through the smoky gloom, I suddenly realized that it was a very old lady. She was bent almost double with age and, when I could make out her face, I saw she looked like a witch from a storybook.

For a moment I almost ran and left her there. The strange unreal atmosphere that the huge fire had brought into the city made anything seem possible, and finding a witch living in an alleyway near Lombard

Street didn't seem anywhere near as unlikely as the country's biggest city going up in flames!

I was so scared I began to shake, but suddenly the old lady looked at me with eyes that were so blue they reminded me of forget-me-nots. They had been my mother's favourite flower, and the thought of her calmed me down a little.

"You're a good boy helping old Mother Bellows," the old lady said. "I've watched many a strong man hurry on by, but it took a youngster like you to stop and save me."

"We're not safe yet, Mother Bellows," I said at last, coming to my senses. "We've got to get you out of here."

Peering through the smoky gloom I saw that there were lots of pieces of furniture lying about. I grabbed what I could and piled them up against the window until I'd made a sort of staircase the old lady could climb.

I don't know how long it took to get up onto the windowsill, but by the time I was able to climb down into the street and then help Mother Bellows down too, the room behind us had started to catch fire.

"I think we need to move out into the middle of the street, if we can," I said as, with a sudden whoosh, the house set ablaze and the window where we'd been standing only moments before was now filled with flames.

We moved with the speed of a tortoise, and when we were far enough away from the blazing house, the old lady turned back to look at it.

"I was born there when the old king's father was still on the throne," she said sadly. "And now it's gone."

"You mean in the time of James I?" I asked, amazed that anyone could've lived that long.

"That's right, but all things come to an end."

"All things but this fire, it seems," I said, watching as the entire row of houses in front of us added more fuel to the flames.

"Oh it'll end too, don't you worry about that," said Mother Bellows. "But I wonder if there'll be anything left of London by the time it does."

....

We slowly made our way down to the River Thames while people rushed by us, pushing handcarts piled high with their belongings and with sacks slung over their backs. Nobody stopped to ask an old lady and young boy if they needed help. It was almost as though we were invisible. The heat from the blaze billowed over and around us in great gusts, and sparks flew through the air like fiery rain, but I felt strangely calm walking quietly with Mother Bellows.

"What are you doing here in the middle of the fire?" the old lady suddenly asked, and it took me a moment or two to remember that I'd been looking for Pip.

"My dog ran away," I answered. "I was trying to find him, but I don't think I will now."

"Oh, you will… or at least he'll find you. He's not hurt, just frightened."

I looked at the tiny lady who stood only as high as my shoulder. "How can you know that?"

She gazed at me calmly and I could see the fire dancing in her blue eyes. "I know," she replied and smiled sweetly.

But before I could ask anything more, a voice interrupted the strange thoughts that were chasing each other around my head.

"Granny! Granny, you're safe! Oh thank goodness."

I looked up to see a girl about my age running up the street towards us, closely followed by a man I thought must be her father.

Mother Bellows smiled as the girl flung herself at her. "We would've been here earlier, but we couldn't get a boat no matter how hard we tried. They've all been hired or won't risk coming in close to the fire!"

"Well, not to worry, I'm safe now, Tilly. Tom here helped me to get out of the house."

"And how is the house, Mother-in-law?" the man asked.

"Gone the way all things that live in this world will go, Jon, to ashes and dust."

Just then I finally noticed that they were all dressed in black clothes with white lace collars. Mother Bellows and the girl, Tilly, both had white linen bonnets that fitted their heads closely, while the man wore a broad-brimmed black hat. They were Puritans!

I'd always been told that Puritans were hard, unfriendly people who spent all their time praying to God, with no time for anything else. But Mother Bellows was a gentle and kindly soul and Tilly seemed very friendly. Even her father, Jon, had nodded to me respectfully when he heard how I'd rescued his mother-in-law.

"Well, we must away, before we're roasted like a chicken or smoked like a kipper by this fire," Jon said. "Will you come with us to find safety, young Tom?"

"Tom has his dog to find, and a lot yet to learn before he returns to his own home," said Mother Bellows.

I smiled and shyly took her hand as I said goodbye. "And don't you worry about Pip," the old lady went on. "He's not meant to die in the flames, but in a good few years from now in the warm arms of a young man who'll miss him when he's finally gone."

And with that the little family of Puritans all waved and moved off down to the Thames. When they were out of sight I felt something draw me to Fleet Street, where Master Pepys and I had been only two days before.

"Pip's out there somewhere, and if Mother Bellows is right, I'll find him." It was as I said the dog's name that I realized I'd never told the old lady what he was called, and yet she'd called him 'Pip' when she told me he'd be safe from the fire. How could she have known?

I turned and peered through the banks of black smoke to see if I could see Mother Bellows, but she was gone.

CHAPTER 7

I ran on down to Fleet Street, trying to make up for lost time. How I thought I could possibly find one little black and white dog in all of that chaos of heat and flames and horrible noise I don't know, but something drove me on. I did see dogs of all shapes and sizes, but none of them were Pip. Some were with their owners tied to carts, or hurrying along on leads, but others were alone and running in terror through the fire. I wished I could have helped them, but there was nothing I could have done.

As I made my way east along the main road, I suddenly saw the huge shape of Saint Paul's Cathedral rising up out of the flames. Its solid stone walls shimmered in the heat haze as though they were made of nothing but water.

I remembered that when I'd been there earlier with Master Pepys the houses to the north and east of the massive church were still safe from the flames, and this seemed as good a reason as any to go that way. Surely Pip would run away from the flames and go towards a place of safety.

I continued along Fleet Street, dodging the carts and crowds of people hurrying down to the Thames, where they obviously hoped to get a boat to take them away to safety. I kept sight of the cathedral on my right and eventually risked turning off the main way and plunging into the narrower streets that led north. Here the fire was fierce, and twice I was driven back by heat and smoke before I found a street that was completely untouched by the flames. In disbelief I walked along between houses that looked as normal as the dirty and narrow streets of London could look. There was even a cat sitting on one of the steps, calmly watching the billowing clouds of smoke as they rolled over the sky.

At last the streets began to open out and I arrived at the wide area that surrounded the cathedral. I couldn't believe my eyes! Everything was now in uproar. When I'd been there earlier with Master Pepys, the building had been covered in scaffolding as workmen carried out repairs to the roof. But now, my God, the whole thing was on fire – it roared and raged in horribly bright and brilliant colours of red and orange set against the smoky black of the sky.

The entire roof was alight – nothing but searing light and terrible scorching heat. I stood with my mouth hanging open and watched as molten lead poured from the roof in a constant stream, like a boiling waterfall. It was so hot it flowed over the ground like silver water and set light to anything that would burn as soon as it touched.

I backed away to a piece of rising ground so the boiling lead couldn't reach me, but then a loud CRACK exploded into the air, and pieces of stone shot around me. CRACK! Another sharp explosion, like a musket being fired, and again, jagged pieces of stone flew around the open area in front of the cathedral. CRACK! This time I saw what was happening; the stones of the cathedral's walls were exploding in the huge heat, peppering the area around with deadly pieces of flying stone, like bullets from a gun.

As I watched, a group of people hurried by pushing a handcart, and just as they were about to dive down into one of the streets that led to the river, another sharp explosion sounded and the man pushing the cart fell with a scream. The rest of the group gathered around and, almost without hesitating, they lifted him onto the cart and hurried on, getting as far away from the cathedral as they could.

This was obviously the best thing to do. Staring through the heat haze and billowing smoke, I could see that Ludgate Hill and part of Cheapside were ablaze, the very areas that I hoped Pip would go to be safe from the fire! So I quickly turned around and hurried away, putting as much distance between me and the boiling lead and exploding stones of the cathedral as I could. I could only hope that Pip had done exactly the same and was safe somewhere.

....

I don't know how long I ran through the burning streets of the city. The sky was dark with clouds of smoke, so I couldn't guess the time and any church bells that still rang the hours had either been burnt down or their chimes were lost in the deafening roar of the fire. I could see no landmarks to guide me and I soon lost my way. One burning street looks much the same as another.

As I ran, I coughed and spluttered in the smoke. My hands were black with soot and I guessed that my face would be in the same state. My clothes were scorched too and peppered with small black holes where sparks had hit me and burned through the cloth. Some of these sparks had reached my skin and I could feel tiny burns all over my back, shoulders, arms and legs.

I knew I couldn't go on for much longer; my chest ached from the smoke and fumes and I could hardly breathe. I had to get out of the fire and find a safe place to rest. Eventually I was forced to slow down by sheer exhaustion until I was barely shuffling forwards, pushed along by the crowds of people who were still cramming the streets as they ran from the fire. Despite feeling totally worn out, I forced myself to keep looking, to keep searching for any sign of Pip. Where was he? Why couldn't I find him? But really I knew it was impossible. I suppose I secretly knew it always had been. How could I have hoped to find one little runaway dog in this huge city? Especially when the city was engulfed in flames?

The fire was closing in on everyone and everything.

It would kill all living things in its path. What chance did any of us have against the fury of the flames?

I had no idea which direction I was heading in, but eventually I began to make out some high stone walls rising above the flames. At first I thought I'd gone round in circles and had somehow made my way back to the cathedral, but then I realized it was the Tower of London! I was closer to home than I had dared hope. If I could see the stone walls I must be at the very beginning of Tower Street, so all I had to do was head north and I'd soon reach Seething Lane where Master Pepys' house stood.

I knew that the house would be empty by now because when I'd run off in search of Pip, the servants had been packing everything up as they prepared to flee from the flames. I had no idea where they were going, either, because I hadn't been told in all the chaos or perhaps I'd forgotten. Maybe the fire had reached Seething Lane and the house would just be a smoking ruin. But I had to go and find out – it was the only link I had with the people who were the closest I had to a family. If it was gone then I really would have nothing in all the world. No home, no friends and, worst of all, no Pip! But I couldn't just give up and turn away. Maybe someone would come back to see if the building had survived the fire and I could ask where everyone had gone.

As soon as I could, I turned north and began to climb up the hill that led down towards the Thames and up towards the City Wall and Aldgate. And very quickly I found myself stepping out of the burning streets and into an area that was untouched by the flames. I was amazed; I'd almost begun to expect to see blazing houses and billows of smoke, as if a city on fire was the way things normally were. Of course there was still the stink of smoke and the loud roar of the inferno, but in every other way these houses seemed safe and sound. Most of them were boarded up because the owners had fled in the belief that the fire would soon reach them. But some were still occupied. As I walked by one of the larger houses, I saw a maid cleaning the smoky grime from the windows as though it was just another working day. My eyes filled with tears when I realized that normal things still happened, but I quickly blinked them away and told myself not to be stupid.

There were still plenty of people crowding the streets even here, but I soon realized that rather than going south to the Thames, they must be heading north, perhaps to Bishops Gate and beyond that to where there was open ground at Moorfields. There were no houses or other buildings there, so the fire couldn't reach them.

I carried on walking, my earlier exhaustion forgotten as I got closer to home. I made my way along a slowly curving street until I came to the foot of Seething Lane, where Master Pepys' house stood. I paused for a moment. With relief I saw that the fire had left the street completely untouched, but I then remembered that no one would be at home. Even so, as I'd thought earlier, perhaps people would come back at regular intervals to check that all was well, and they'd find me.

But as I walked up the lane, I began to wonder if I was still Master Pepys' pageboy at all. After all, I'd abandoned him and run off at a time when I was needed to help pack up the house and take everything to safety. Perhaps I'd been sacked and was now just another boy living on the streets of London. Even if my master did come back, would he just be angry and send me away?

My steps slowed as I thought this through, but as I had nowhere else to go I eventually picked up my pace again and hurried on. Perhaps Master Pepys would forgive me and let me work in the kitchens again, even if he didn't want me as a pageboy anymore.

Then at long last I saw the house. It stood as it always had in a small plot of land with a low wall around it. To the side was the tiny orchard with three apple and two pear trees where I used to take Pip first thing in the morning. I was overcome with sadness as I remembered my little black and white dog and wondered where he was and if he was still alive. Then I recalled what old Mother Bellows had said about him being safe and I decided to cheer up. But not for long. As I ran my eyes over the house I noticed that all of the windows had their shutters firmly closed and the great double front door was also shut and looked as solid and as unmoveable as stone.

Even the gates to the garden were padlocked, but it was easy to scramble over the wall and into the orchard. I found my way to the biggest apple tree and sat down staring at the house. My eyes were really heavy and I suddenly realized that I didn't know exactly how long I'd been in the fire searching for Pip. It could have been a few hours or it could have been more than a day.

Above the blazing houses the sky was black with smoke and so it was impossible to know if the day had ended and a new one had begun. I could've been awake for more than a day and a night!

I lay back against the trunk of the tree and closed my eyes. I don't know how long I slept, but I woke up just as I was dreaming that someone was wiping the soot off my face with a wet cloth. In fact the dream was so real that even as I opened my eyes I could still feel the wet cloth scrubbing at my cheek.

I put my hands up to my wet face and felt something solid that whined and then gave a little yap.

....

I tried to focus my sleepy eyes. "PIP!" I screamed and seized the dog who began licking my face again. "PIP! You're safe! Where have you been? Where did you get to?! I've been looking for you for… for… well I don't know for how long!"

Pip barked excitedly and then licked my face again. I laughed and hugged him close, and we were both so happy that neither of us heard the person approaching.

Suddenly someone grabbed my shoulder in a strong grip and spun me round.

I gasped and stared up into the face of... Master Pepys. His eyes bulged and his wig slipped to one side as he glared at me. I just knew I'd been sacked!

Terrified I immediately began to gabble explanations and excuses: "I'm sorry... I didn't mean to run away... I was looking for Pip... I was afraid he'd die in the fire..."

Master Pepys said nothing but suddenly gathered us both in a huge hug. "Thank God, thank God, my two best boys are safe!" he said and laughed aloud.

I was amazed; I thought we were going to be beaten, and yet here he was laughing and behaving as though he really cared what happened to us. Not only that, but I had no idea he even knew Pip existed. The little dog spent most of his time in the kitchens and cellars where my master rarely went.

For the next few minutes I tried to explain everything that had been happening. I had to pick up Master Pepys' wig from the dusty ground twice and replace it on his head, while he continued to smile at us, like – as he said himself – "A man who'd lost a crust of bread and found a roast chicken instead."

But then at last he seemed to remember he should be angry with us and, after a few tries, he managed to make his face look stern and told us that we'd both get a beating later for running away. Pip obviously didn't believe him and yapped until Master Pepys finally picked him up and had his face washed too.

"Come now, into the house both of you to get clean and fed and ready for the new day ahead," he said, leading the way to the locked front doors.

"But is there any food left in the house? Hasn't everything been taken to safety?" I asked, suddenly realizing how very hungry I was.

"You're right, Tom. There's not a crumb to be found anywhere inside. But fortunately I brought a basket of goodies with me in case I got peckish during my visit to check on things."

CHAPTER 8

The fire died at last, though it died slowly, and throughout Thursday reports came in that it had been stopped at several points. I didn't know it at the time of course, but its defeat began on Wednesday while I was still searching for Pip. High brick walls at Middle Temple and also at Fetter Lane had stopped it moving north and firebreaks at Cripplegate, Smithfield and Holborn Bridge prevented it from destroying any more homes and lives.

It's been claimed by the government that only six people died, but nobody believes that. Some say that the authorities have only bothered to count those they think important – in other words, the rich, the aristocracy and those with power. But I remember the screams and cries as I walked through the burning streets, and I believe many more died in the flames. When the Great Plague killed thousands of people, their bodies were left as evidence. But the fire burnt its victims to ash and unrecognizable charred cinders that could be ignored and shovelled away with the other debris as the clear-up began.

That morning I stood on my bed and looked out of the window in the roof of the attic bedroom I shared with Pip. I held the little dog in my arms so that we could both see the still-smoking ruins that spread far to the east towards Holborn Hill and south to the Thames in the early morning light.

"Look, Pip, it's stopped. We're safe and we still have a place in Master Pepys' home. We're lucky, though there are thousands that'll be sleeping under the skies tonight and for many more nights to come."

Pip yapped as though he understood, but then he wriggled to be put down and we both headed for the stairs to start our day.

After breakfast Master Pepys decided he wanted to see the ruins "at first hand". We set out to walk towards the blackened and broken walls of Saint Paul's Cathedral that towered in the distance over the debris of what had once been a large part of the city. I'd been told that eighty-four churches had been destroyed as well as more than 13,000 houses. But those numbers gave no real idea about the people whose lives had been ruined. Many had lost their businesses – the only way they had of making a living and feeding themselves and their families. Someone in the government had calculated that more than 100,000 were now homeless, with very little hope of getting anywhere else to live.

This made me think of Mother Bellows, the old Puritan lady I'd helped, but at least I thought she'd be safe with her family, unlike some who might have nobody to help them.

In the end all I could do was accept that I could do nothing to help; I was just a twelve-year-old boy who had the good fortune to work for a kind master in a good household and I quietly breathed a sigh of relief. In fact, I was soon back into the routine of being a pageboy and, as Master Pepys and I made our way towards the ruins of the burnt streets, I walked two paces behind him, carrying his finely embroidered gloves.

Everything was deadly quiet where once there'd been the hustle and bustle of a busy city. But even so there were many people about, picking their way through the ruined houses. I thought that perhaps they were looking for where their homes had once stood, but many of them just seemed dazed and wandered about aimlessly.

We walked on for what seemed like hours and, even though the fire was now definitely out, the ruins still smoked and gave off heat and sparks in great billowing clouds.

There were rumours that the fire had been started deliberately by the country's enemies, but my master didn't believe it:

"Accident, Tom, pure accident," he said, when I asked him. "It's said that a bakery in Pudding Lane didn't put out its ovens properly and that a spark escaped and set fire to rubbish and from there it spread." He fell silent for a moment before adding. "There's a lesson to be learnt from that, my boy… from a tiny spark of mischief can come the greatest of tragedies."

I nodded, but said nothing as we arrived before the huge broken remains of Saint Paul's Cathedral. Some of its walls still stood, but they were blackened and there were great holes where the stones had exploded in the heat. It was also completely roofless and the great central tower had fallen in, leaving nothing but a smoking shell.

"Even the houses of God have been destroyed," I said quietly.

Master Pepys laid his hand on my shoulder. "But they will rise again, my lad. They will rise again. Already the king is calling for plans that will allow a great re-building of all that has been lost. But this time it will be better. It will be built of stone and of brick so that no fire will ever again burn our city…"

....

That night as I lay in my bed, I told Pip what Master Pepys had said and he yapped as though agreeing with every word. We went to sleep, safe in the knowledge that our city would never burn again.

HISTORICAL NOTE

The Great Fire of London started at one o'clock in the morning on Sunday 2nd September 1666 in a baker's shop that stood on a street called Pudding Lane. By seven o'clock the same morning, Samuel Pepys was woken by his maid to be told that over three hundred houses had already been burnt down.

Pepys decided that the king must be told about the situation and at ten o'clock he travelled to the Palace of Whitehall. He told Charles II about the terrible fire and recommended that houses should be pulled down to stop it spreading further. The king agreed and sent Pepys to tell the Lord Mayor, Thomas Bloodworth, to demolish all buildings in the path of the flames.

By one o'clock in the morning of Monday 3rd September, the fire had spread and the post office on Cloak Lane was destroyed. The postmaster and his family had to run for their lives, taking as much post with them as they could carry. The king's brother, the Duke of York, was put in charge of the efforts to stop the fire and he called in the army to help in the fight against the flames.

But many other people helped too; the headmaster of Westminster School led his schoolboys in a successful battle to save the church of Saint Dunstan-in-the-East. Even so, the fire continued to spread and by nine o'clock a huge area of the city has been destroyed and the flames were less than 300 metres away from the Tower of London. The king then ordered as many fire-engines as could be spared to save it.

By this time hundreds of houses, dozens of churches and even Baynard's Castle had been destroyed by the flames. Then on 4th September the area of Cheapside – one of the richest streets in the entire city – caught fire. The king's mother, Henrietta Maria, was forced to leave her home and seek safety in the palace of Hampton Court.

More and more houses, churches and official buildings were burnt to the ground, and then at eight o'clock in the evening, the huge Saint Paul's Cathedral caught fire and was destroyed.

Early the next morning on September 5th, Samuel Pepys fled from his house in Seething Lane and went to Woolwich. But then, at last, a fire at Holborn Bridge was successfully put out and by seven o'clock that evening all fires in the west of the city were extinguished, apart from one in an area called Cripplegate.

The next day at five o'clock in the morning, Pepys led a group of sailors to fight a blaze in Bishops Gate. This was the last outbreak of the fire and by the next day, September 7th 1666, the Great Fire of London was finally out.

Now began the process of clearing away the debris of all the destroyed buildings, and on September 11th the architect Sir Christopher Wren presented plans to the king for the rebuilding of the city. His crowning achievement would be the new Saint Paul's Cathedral, which would rise again from the ashes.

By November 20th the streets of London were cleared of all debris and the rebuilding could begin. Even so, many people had lost their homes and their businesses and it would be years before the re-building was completed. How long the process would take can be seen in the fact that the new Saint Paul's Cathedral wasn't re-opened for worship until 2nd December 1697, thirty-two years and three months after the Great Fire that had destroyed the earlier building.

But the greatest cost could have been the people who died in the flames. Official figures claimed that only six people were killed in the fire, but some historians believe that the numbers of fatalities must have been far higher. Reports at the time simply didn't record the deaths of ordinary working class people.

In addition to this, some figures have claimed that as many as 100,000 people were left homeless as thousands of houses were destroyed. Alhough temporary shelters were built, they were of poor quality and it's believed that large numbers of people would have died of the cold in the harsh winter that followed the fire.

Many shops and other businesses were also destroyed by the flames, which meant countless people lost their jobs and their ability to earn money. This led to extreme poverty at a time when there were very few organised ways to help them.

EXPERIENCE HISTORY FIRST-HAND WITH *MY STORY* – A SERIES OF VIVIDLY IMAGINED ACCOUNTS OF LIFE IN THE PAST.

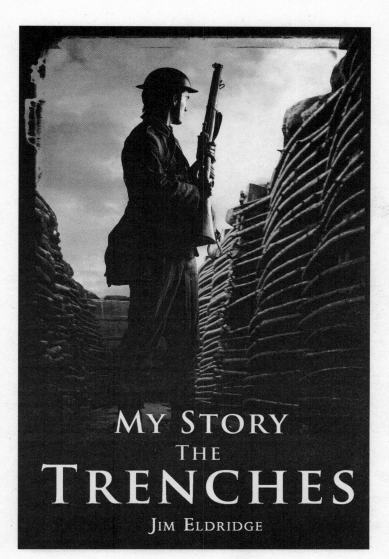

MY STORY
THE
TRENCHES

JIM ELDRIDGE

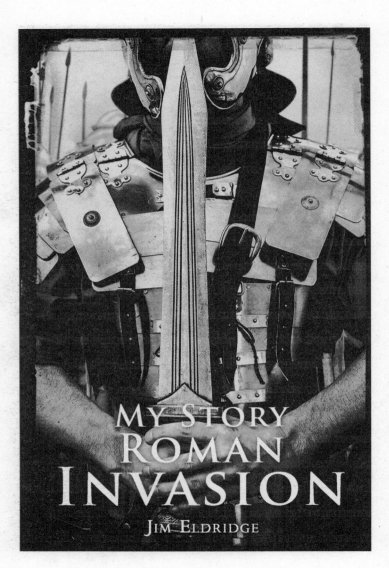

My Story
Roman
INVASION

Jim Eldridge

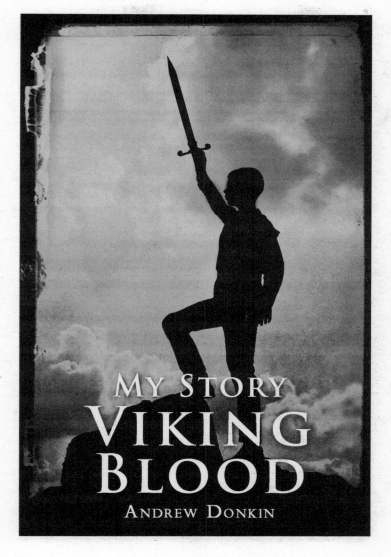

MY STORY
VIKING
BLOOD

ANDREW DONKIN

MY STORY
D-DAY

BRYAN PERRETT